The Worrywarts

Pamela Duncan Edwards • illustrated by Henry Cole

HarperCollinsPublishers

For Carron Machar Pickett, my niece,
wishing her all the wonders of the world.
—P.D.E.

A warm welcome to Alexander Mazon,
wishing you well as you wander through the world!
—H.C.

THE WORRYWARTS

Text copyright © 1999 by Pamela Edwards
Illustrations copyright © 1999 by Henry Cole
ISBN 0-06-028150-2. — ISBN 0-06-028149-9 (lib. bdg.)
Library of Congress catalog card number: 98-47503
Printed in the U.S.A. All rights reserved.
http://www.harperchildrens.com
Typography by Elynn Cohen and Michele Tupper
3 4 5 6 7 8 9 10
❖

The Worrywarts

One warm Wednesday morning, the sun winked through Wombat's window and woke her up.

"What a wonderful day to wander the world," she thought.

Wombat went to ask Weasel and Woodchuck whether they would go with her.

"Where *is* the world?" asked Weasel.

"Past the wishing well, down the pathway, and through the woods," answered Woodchuck, who was very well-read.

So they set to work, wondering what to take with them.

Wombat wanted watercress-on-whole-wheat-bread sandwiches, walnut wafers, waffles with whipped cream, wedges of watermelon, and her walking stick.

Weasel wanted wieners and liverwurst, and his water pistol.

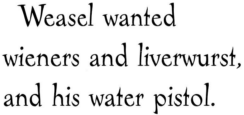

Woodchuck wanted the "W" volume of *Webster's Book of Words*, in case they needed to look up information about "The World."

But then Wombat began to worry. "WAIT!" she wailed.

"WHAT IF . . .

. . . we're walking past the wallflowers and a swarm of wasps is waiting? What if they swirl around us and we've nothing to swat them with?

"What if
we're running away
and we're not
watching where we're going and suddenly we're
wading up to our waists in water? What if a
wave whooshes over us and a wallowing
walrus swims up and swallows us?

"WHAT THEN?"

"If we're going swimming," said Weasel, "I'll want to wear my water wings!"

"You're so wise, Weasel," cried Wombat. "We won't be worrywarts!"

But then Weasel began to worry. "WAIT!" he wailed.

"WHAT IF . . .

. . . we're waltzing down the pathway when a wicked wolf comes winding his way toward us? What if we wave to him but he won't wag his tail?

"What if we're running away when the weather worsens? What if a whirlwind blows in from the west and sweeps us away into the wilderness?

"WHAT THEN?"

"If it's going to be windy," said Woodchuck, "I'll want to wear my woolly underwear!"

"You're so wise, Woodchuck," cried Weasel. "We won't be worrywarts."

But then Woodchuck began to worry. "WAIT!" he wailed.

"WHAT IF . . .

. . . we're whistling while we walk through the woods and we wake up an owl? What if he gets worked up and swoops down with a swish of his wings and whisks us away?

"What if the weight's too much for him and he begins to wobble? What if he drops us into a swamp and a warthog comes waddling along and wallops us?

"WHAT THEN?"

"If we're going flying," said Wombat, "I'll want to wear my wind helmet!"

"You're so wise, Wombat," cried Woodchuck. "We won't be worrywarts."

Then, without wasting any more time, they wrapped
the watercress-on-whole-wheat-bread sandwiches,

the waffles with whipped cream,

the walnut wafers,

the wedges of watermelon,

and the wieners and
liverwurst in waxed paper.

Woodchuck put the "W" volume of *Webster's Book of Words*
into his wheelbarrow, and away they went to wander the world.

After a while, Wombat said,
"I was wondering whether we
should eat our sandwiches?"

So they sat on a
wall. They played with a
wiggly worm and watched
a spider weaving a web
on the wisteria.

But suddenly,
"WATCH OUT!"
warned a woodpecker from
a weeping willow tree.

Something whooshed
around Wombat's watercress-
on-whole-wheat-bread
sandwiches.

"A wasp!" she cried.

Swiftly, Wombat whacked
the air with her walking
stick and whizzed a wedge
of watermelon into some
weeds.

"Wow!" whooped the wasp.
"Watermelon! Mouthwatering!"
And the wasp went winging away.
"Well done, Wombat!" cried
Weasel and Woodchuck.
"You were wonderful!"
"You're welcome," said Wombat,
and they set off again to wander
the world.

But suddenly, "WATCH OUT!" came a whisper from a rabbit warren. Someone came swaggering down the pathway toward them.

"Whoops!" cried Weasel. "A wicked wolf!" Swiftly, Weasel twirled his wieners and liverwurst into some wildflowers and swooshed his water pistol at the wolf.

"Weiners and liverwurst!" cried the wolf, wiping his wet whiskers. "I'm wild about wieners and liverwurst!"

Away he went with his tail wagging. "Way to go!" cried Wombat and Woodchuck. "You were very wily, Weasel!"

"We weren't wimps," agreed Weasel, and they set off again to wander the world.

But suddenly, "WATCH OUT!"
warbled a wagtail. Woodchuck saw
an eye twinkling behind a twig.

"An owl!" he cried.

Swiftly, Woodchuck whirled his
"W" volume of *Webster's Book of
Words* at the owl. *WHANG!*

"Whoopee!" cried the owl. "Just what I wanted to help me win my word game!"

"You're so wise, Woodchuck," said Wombat and Weasel.

"We've walked a long way," said Wombat.

"I'm weak and weary," said Weasel.

"I'm worn out," said Woodchuck.

So they went back along the pathway.

"When will we wander the world again?" wondered Wombat.

"I wish we could go again next week," said Weasel.

"Why not?" said Woodchuck.

"BUT . . .

WHAT IF . . . ? ”

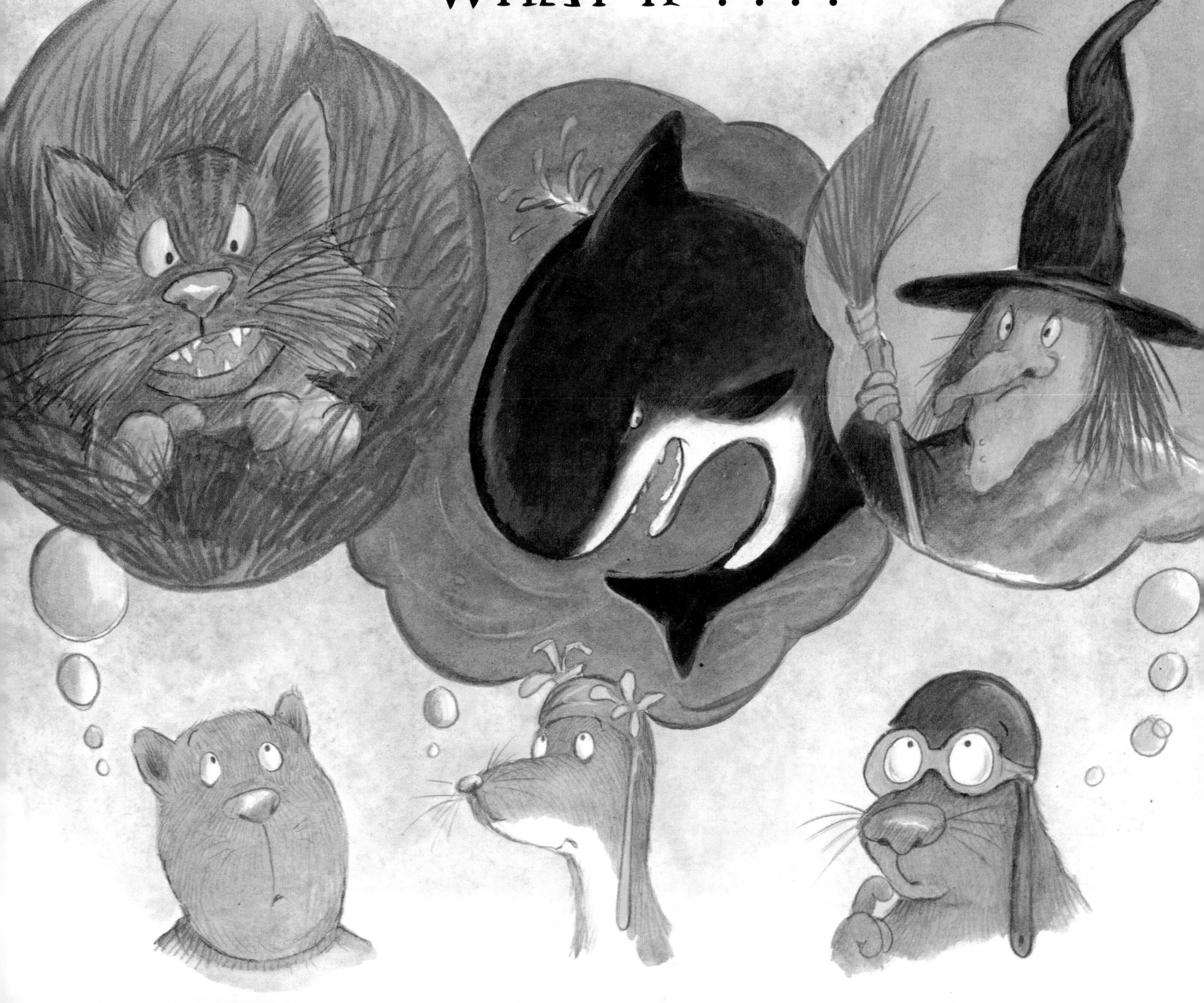